Parents and Caregivers,

Stone Arch Readers are designed to provide enjoyable reading experiences, as well as opportunities to develop vocabulary, literacy skills, and comprehension. Here are a few ways to support your beginning reader:

- Talk with your child about the ideas addressed in the story.

- Discuss each illustration, mentioning the characters, where they are, and what they are doing.

- Read with expression, pointing to each word. You may want to read the whole story through and then revisit parts of the story to ensure that the meanings of words or phrases are understood.

- Talk about why the character did what he or she did and what your child would do in that situation.

- Help your child connect with characters and events in the story.

Remember, reading with your child should be fun, not forced. Each moment spent reading with your child is a priceless investment in his or her literacy life.

Gail Saunders-Smith, Ph.D.

STONE ARCH READERS

are published by Stone Arch Books, a Capstone Imprint
1710 Roe Crest Drive
North Mankato, Minnesota 56003
www.capstonepub.com

Library of Congress Cataloging-in-Publication Data

Klein, Adria F. (Adria Fay), 1947-

City Train / by Adria Klein ; illustrated by Craig Cameron.

p. cm. -- (Stone Arch readers: Train time)

Summary: City Train picks up people from all the stations
and takes them into the city.

ISBN 978-1-4342-4189-4 (library binding)

ISBN 978-1-4342-4884-8 (pbk.)

1. Railroad trains--Juvenile fiction. [1. Railroad trains--Fiction.]
I. Cameron, Craig, ill. II. Title.

PZ7.K678324Cit 2013

[E]--dc23

2012026289

Reading Consultants:

Gail Saunders-Smith, Ph.D.

Melinda Melton Crow, M.Ed.

Laurie K. Holland, Media Specialist

Designer: Russell Griesmer

Printed in the United States of America in Stevens Point, Wisconsin.

092012   006937WZS13

City
Train

written by
Adria F. Klein

illustrated by
Craig Cameron

STONE ARCH BOOKS
a capstone imprint

City Train went to work.

She stopped at a train station.

"I am ready," she said.

She got some people.

She went over a bridge.

She got more people.

15

She went through a tunnel.

She got more people.

She went around a lake.

She got more people.

Then she stopped in the city.

"Toot! Toot!" she said.

All the people got off.

"What a busy day!" she said.

STORY WORDS

station   bridge   lake

people   tunnel

Word Count: 68

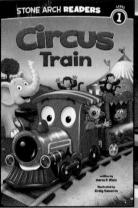

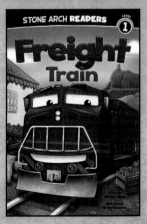